Dame
Dearlove's Ditties
for the Nursery

HISTORICAL NOTE

Dame Dearlove's Ditties for the Nursery; so Wonderfully Contrived, that they may be either Sung or Said by Nurse or Baby appeared in 1819, being a selection from an earlier title from 1805, *Original Ditties for the Nursery*. This new version is a selection from the 1819 collection.

Dame Dearlove's Ditties for the Nursery

illustrated by
RODNEY McRAE

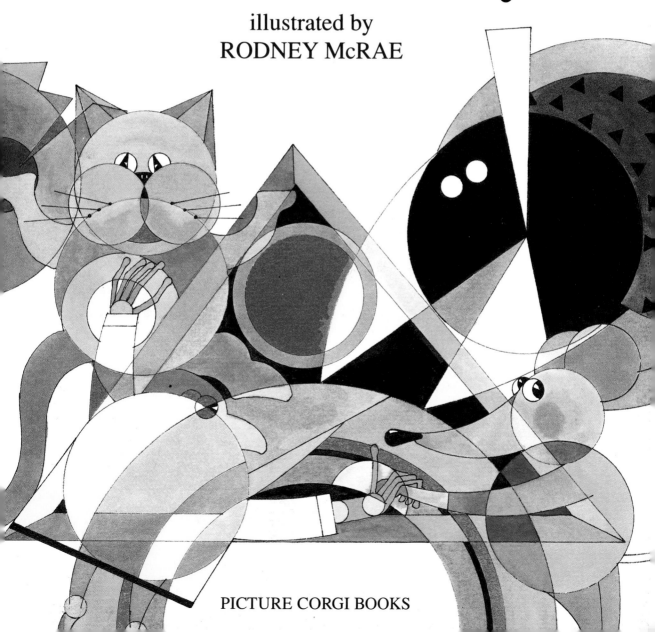

PICTURE CORGI BOOKS

Squire Frog's Visit

Squire Frog he went to Mouse's hall,
  "Heigh ho!" says Brittle;
Squire Frog he went to Mouse's hall,
Dressed out quite smart for a supper and ball;
  With a namby, pamby,
  Mannikin, pannikin,
"Heigh!" says Barnaby Brittle.

Mr Rat he bowed, and welcomed him in,
  "Heigh ho!" says Brittle;
Mr Rat he bowed, and welcomed him in,
And all the Miss Mouses went curtseying;
  With a namby, pamby,
  Mannikin, pannikin,
"Heigh!" says Barnaby Brittle.

3

Then Rat did for the fiddles call,
  "Heigh ho!" says Brittle;
Then Rat did for the fiddles call,
And requested that Froggy would open the ball;
  With a namby, pamby,
  Mannikin, pannikin,
"Heigh!" says Barnaby Brittle.

4

They danced until the clock struck one,
"Heigh ho!" says Brittle;
They danced until the clock struck one,
When Rat said supper was begun;
With a namby, pamby,
Mannikin, pannikin,
"Heigh!" says Barnaby Brittle.

5

"Good wife, pray hand that dish below,"
  "Heigh ho!" says Brittle;
"Good wife, pray hand that dish below,
For Froggy and I love harico;"
  With a namby, pamby,
  Mannikin, pannikin,
"Heigh!" says Barnaby Brittle.

6

"Go fetch the wine from off the hob,"
  "Heigh ho!" says Brittle;
"Go fetch the wine from off the hob,
For Froggy and I must hob or nob;"
  With a namby, pamby,
  Mannikin, pannikin,
"Heigh!" says Barnaby Brittle.

7

Then Frog he begged to give a toast,
  "Heigh ho!" says Brittle;
Then Frog he begged to give a toast,
"May the French never fricassee me on our
    coast."
  With a namby, pamby,
  Mannikin, pannikin,
"Heigh!" says Barnaby Brittle.

8

Whilst thus they merry-making sat,
 "Heigh ho!" says Brittle;
Whilst thus they merry-making sat,
Came bouncing in the great black cat;
 With a namby, pamby,
 Mannikin, pannikin,
"Heigh!" says Barnaby Brittle.

She seized the old rat in a trice,
  "Heigh ho!" says Brittle;
She seized the old rat in a trice,
And vengeance vowed on all the mice;
  With a namby, pamby,
  Mannikin, pannikin,
"Heigh!" says Barnaby Brittle.

When Froggy saw their dismal plight,
  "Heigh ho!" says Brittle;
When Froggy saw their dismal plight,
He thought it wiser to wish them good-night;
  With a namby, pamby,
  Mannikin, pannikin,
"Heigh!" says Barnaby Brittle.

11

The Heroes

Tweedledum and Tweedledee,
    Agreed to fight a battle;
For Tweedledum, said Tweedledee,
    Had spoiled his nice new rattle.

14

Just then flew down a monstrous crow,
As black as a tar barrel;
Which frightened both those heroes so,
They quite forgot their quarrel.

The Old Woman and Her Cat

There was an old woman, who rode on a broom,
  With a high gee ho! gee humble;
And she took her Tom Cat behind for a groom,
  With a bimble, bamble, bumble.

16

They travelled along till they came to the sky,
  With a high gee ho! gee humble;
But the journey so long made them very hungry,
  With a bimble, bamble, bumble.

Says Tom, "I can find nothing here to eat,
   With a high gee ho! gee humble;
So let us go back again, I entreat,
   With a bimble, bamble, bumble."

The old woman would not go back so soon,
  With a high gee ho! gee humble;
For she wanted to visit the man in the moon,
  With a bimble, bamble, bumble.

Says Tom, "I'll go back by myself to our house,
  With a high gee ho! gee humble;
For there I can catch a good rat or a mouse,
  With a bimble, bamble, bumble."

"But," says the old woman, "how will you go?
  With a high gee ho! gee humble,
You shan't have my nag, I protest and vow,
  With a bimble, bamble, bumble."

21

"No, no," says old Tom, "I've a plan of my own,
  With a high gee ho! gee humble,"
So he slid down the rainbow, and left her alone,
  With a bimble, bamble, bumble.

So now if you happen to visit the sky,
  With a high gee ho! gee humble;
And want to come back, you Tom's method may try,
  With a bimble, bamble, bumble.

Robin Hood

Pray who did kill that noble stag?
"'Twas I! 'Twas I! 'Twas I!
And I am called bold Robin Hood!"
Bold Robin, you must die.

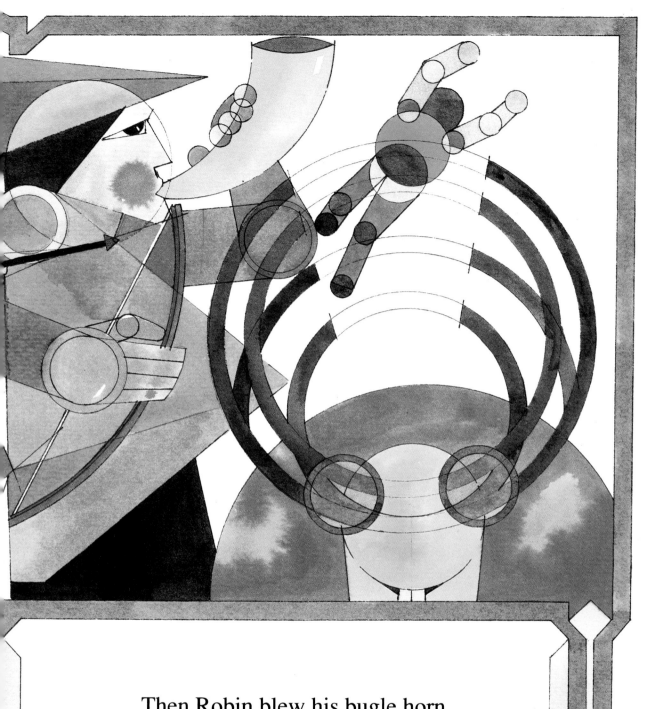

Then Robin blew his bugle horn,
And straight his archers came;
They ducked the verderer in a pool,
And laughed to see his shame.

The Naughty Magpie

A farmer went trotting upon his grey mare,
  Bumpety, bumpety, bump!
With his daughter behind him so rosy and fair;
  Lumpety, lumpety, lump!

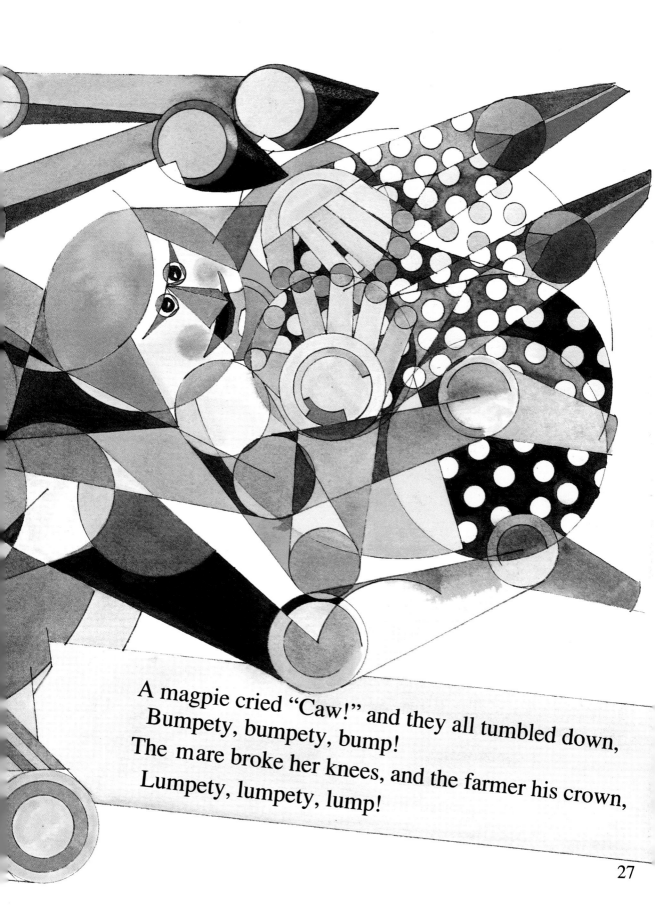

A magpie cried "Caw!" and they all tumbled down,
Bumpety, bumpety, bump!
The mare broke her knees, and the farmer his crown,
Lumpety, lumpety, lump!

The mischievous magpie flew laughing away,
Bumpety, bumpety, bump!
And vowed he would serve them the same the next day,
Lumpety, lumpety, lump!

GLOSSARY

page 6

harico – a stew, usually made with mutton or lamb

page 7

hob – a shelf around a fireplace

page 8

fricasee – to stew and serve with a sauce

page 25

verderer – gamekeeper

DAME DEARLOVE'S DITTIES FOR THE NURSERY
A PICTURE CORGI 0 552 525847

PRINTING HISTORY
First publication in Great Britain 1989
Published simultaneously by Dell, a division of Transworld Publishers
(Australia) Pty Ltd, 1989
Originated and developed by Margaret Hamilton Books Pty Ltd

Picture Corgi Books are published by Transworld Publishers Ltd.,
61-63 Uxbridge Road, Ealing, London W5 5SA.

Made and printed in Singapore by Kyodo-Shing Loong Printing
Industries Pte Ltd